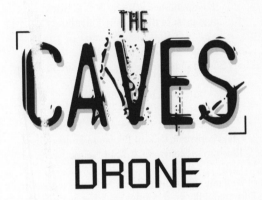

THE
CAVES
DRONE

First published 2014 by A & C Black,
an imprint of Bloomsbury Publishing Plc
50 Bedford Square
London WC1B 3DP
Bloomsbury is a registered trademark of Bloomsbury Publishing Plc

www.bloomsbury.com

ISBN 978-1-4729-0096-8

A CIP catalogue for this book is available from the British Library.

Printed and bound in India by Replika Press Pvt Ltd

1 3 5 7 9 10 8 6 4 2

THE CAVES

DRONE

BENJAMIN HULME-CROSS

Illustrated by
Nelson Evergreen

A & C BLACK
AN IMPRINT OF BLOOMSBURY
LONDON NEW DELHI NEW YORK SYDNEY

The Teens can choose prison for life … or they can go on a game show called The Caves.

If the Teens beat the robot monsters, they go free. If they lose, they die.

I am Zak. Sometimes I help the Teens. Sometimes I don't.

The Teens were called Jay and Olly. They were scared, but they were laughing too. They ran to the caves.

The Voice spoke.

"The game begins in 10 minutes."

"We can kill the monster," said Olly.

"Just like we killed that girl," said Jay.

I thought, "I won't help these Teens."

I went outside.

A drone flew over the rocks. It had cameras for eyes. It had lots of guns.

The Teens had no chance.

"What will they do?" I thought. "Will they run, or fight?"

I climbed into a tunnel and crawled up to the top of the caves.

I looked down.

The Teens stood in the middle of the biggest cave.

They were shouting at each other.

"This is your fault! We didn't have to kill that girl!" Olly shouted. "We could have run away!"

"We had to kill her. She saw you rob the shop!"
Jay shouted back.

"No! We could have run away," shouted Olly.
"And now we're going to die because you don't
know when to fight and when to run."

Jay hit Olly.

Olly kicked Jay in the head.

They knew how to fight!

The Teens didn't hear the drone. They rolled on the ground and hit each other.

Olly got on top. He had his hands on Jay's neck.

The drone flew into the cave.

Jay saw it. But he couldn't speak.
Olly was choking him.

Jay pointed at the drone.

The guns pointed at the Teens. There were two short bangs.

The Voice said,
"Game over!"

Read more of

THE CAVES

SERIES

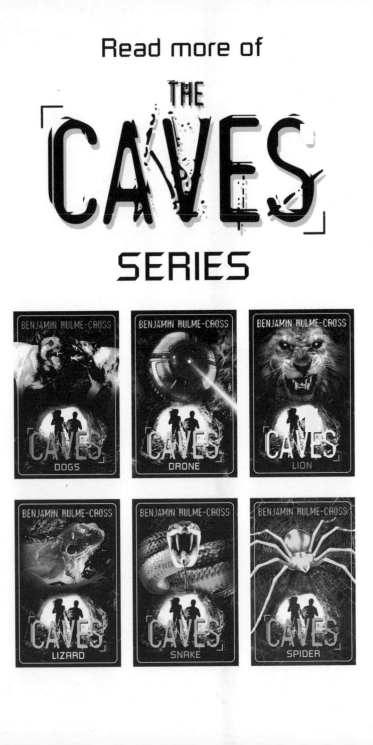